The Dead Sea Squirrels Series

THE DEAD SEA SQUIRRELS

BabbleLand Breakout

Mike Nawrocki

Illustrated by Luke Séguin-Magee

Tyndale House Publishers
Carol Stream, Illinois

Visit Tyndale's website for kids at tyndale.com/kids.

Visit the author's website at mikenawrocki.com.

Tyndale is a registered trademark of Tyndale House Ministries. The Tyndale Kids logo is a trademark of Tyndale House Ministries.

The Dead Sea Squirrels is a registered trademark of Michael L. Nawrocki.

BabbleLand Breakout

Designed by Libby Dykstra

Edited by Deborah King

Published in association with the literary agency of Brentwood Press, P.O. Box 132, Arrington, TN 37014.

Unless otherwise indicated, all Scripture quotations are taken from the *Holy Bible*, New Living Translation, copyright © 1996, 2004, 2015 by Tyndale House Foundation. Used by permission of Tyndale House Publishers, Carol Stream, Illinois 60188. All rights reserved.

Scripture quotation in chapter 10 is taken from the Holy Bible, *New International Version,*® NIV.® Copyright © 1973, 1978, 1984, 2011 by Biblica, Inc.® Used by permission. All rights reserved worldwide.

For manufacturing information regarding this product, please call 1-855-277-9400.

For information about special discounts for bulk purchases, please contact Tyndale House Publishers at csresponse@tyndale.com, or call 1-855-277-9400.

Library of Congress Cataloging-in-Publication Data
A catalog record for this book is available from the Library of Congress.

ISBN 978-1-4964-4993-1

Printed in the United States of America

29	28	27	26	25	24	23
7	6	5	4	3	2	1

To Debbie, Libby, Linda, and Luke—
my dream team editor, designer, publisher,
and illustrator. Thank you for making this
series possible. I will always be grateful for
your amazing talents, trust, and vision.

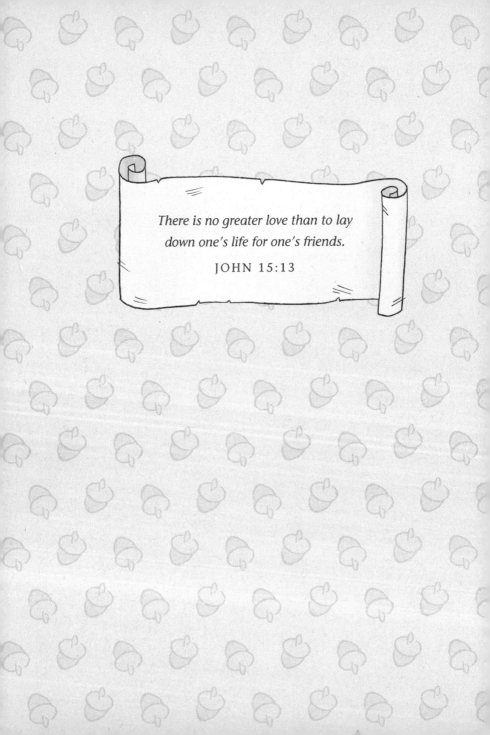

*There is no greater love than to lay
down one's life for one's friends.*

JOHN 15:13

1,950 YEARS LATER Ten-year-old Michael Gomez is spending the summer at the Dead Sea with his professor dad and his best friend, Justin.

While exploring a cave (without his dad's permission), Michael discovers two dried-out, salt-covered critters and stashes them in his backpack.

Michael sneaks the squirrels back home with him to Tennessee.

He sets them up like posable action figures on his dresser—
under an open window.

While Michael is sleeping, a thunderstorm rolls in, and it begins to rain . . .

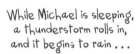

. . . rehydrating the squirrels!

Up and kicking again after almost 2,000 years, Merle and Pearl Squirrel have great stories and advice to share with the modern world.

They are the Dead Sea Squirrels!

But the Dead Sea Squirrels' adventures don't end there. Merle and Pearl soon find out that things are **a whole lot different** from the first century!

For one thing, there are self-filling fresh water bowls . . .

an endless supply of walnuts and chicken nuggets . . .

Thank you, chickens, for your nuggets!

and much fancier places to live!

I could get used to this!

Plus, they get to go to fifth grade (as long as no one sees them)!

Stay still, Merle! Pretend you are stuffed!

But even in quiet Walnut Creek, Tennessee, danger is never too far away!

Nice kitty...

What if Mom and Dad find out?!

And a man in a suit and sunglasses who wants nothing more than to get his hands on the squirrels ... does!

HELP!!!

Now it's back to the Holy Land to rescue the squirrels!

MICHAEL!

CHAPTER 1

Under the cool light of a full moon,
a lone alpaca galloped majestically
through the Israeli countryside.

"Can't . . . you . . . run . . . a little
. . . less . . . bouncy?!" Merle the squirrel hollered in spurts as he clung to
Adriana's tail, very unmajestically.

"Get closer to the withers!" his wife,
Pearl, yelled back from her perch at
the base of the alpaca's neck. "It's
much smoother up here!"

"What's . . . a . . . withers?!"

"It's where I'm sitting!" Pearl replied.
The *withers* of a four-legged animal
means the ridge between the shoulder
blades. If you've ever been on a school

bus, you might have noticed it's a much smoother ride in the front than it is in the back. It's the same with alpacas.

"I prefer the view from up here!" Dave the Lizard of Judah called down from his seat between Adriana's ears, his thin, light frame slicing through the wind.

a.) School Bus

BUMPIER RIDE

SMOOTHER RIDE

b.) Alpaca.

"Hmm . . ." Adriana replied. Not being an animal who could speak human, it's all she ever said.

"You getting tired, girl?" Pearl asked, perfectly understanding the tone of her friend's hum. "Why don't we stop and rest for a while?"

"Hmm . . ." Adriana agreed. She screeched to a stop, sending the head-mounted lizard flying.

"AHHHHH!" Dave screamed before landing with a thud on the sandy soil.

Adriana and Pearl had not slept in the last 24 hours. After narrowly escaping Delilah and Ruben the previous evening in Nazareth, they had traveled over 20 miles to find Merle and Dave on the southern shore of the Sea of Galilee. From there, they struck out immediately on a rescue mission to save their friends—the Gomezes, Justin, Sadie, Dusty, and Ham—who were headed toward BabbleLand and the crooked clutches of Dr. Simon.

"Attagirl! We can't run all the way to Jerusalem without resting," Pearl said. Her plan was to follow the now-familiar path south along the Jordan River to Jericho, and from there to take the Old Jericho Road west to Jerusalem— another 100 miles in total.

"It's almost sunrise," Merle noted. A faint red glow shone on the horizon to the east. "I say we sleep during the day and travel at night."

"Good thinking," Dave replied, dusting himself off. "Fewer harriers to worry about." The previous day, Merle and Dave had barely escaped being eaten by hungry harrier chicks,

whose parents hunt exclusively during
the day.

"And fewer people too," Pearl added.

Merle slid down from Adriana's back
next to Dave. "Why don't Dave and
I take first watch and find some food
while you and Adriana rest?"
he offered.

"That sounds lovely,
dear." Pearl yawned
before curling up
with Adriana in the
safety and shade
of a bushy
palm tree
near the
river.

CHAPTER 2

Good morning and welcome to BabbleLand!

Dr. Simon announced, tapping his fingers together sinisterly as Ruben pulled the church van into the entrance of the nearly finished theme park. Inside sat his captives: Dr. and Mrs. Gomez, Michael, Jane, Justin, and Sadie, sore and bleary-eyed from sleeping in the van that night. Donkeys Dusty and Ham stood in the cart hitched behind.

"Scratch, schmooze, snack, and smile!" Dr. Simon continued as he slid the side door open.

7

"That's really your slogan?" Justin asked, unimpressed.

"The only zoo where cuddly creatures talk to you!" Dr. Simon tried out another line.

Sadie shrugged. "Maybe a little better? I like the rhyme, but the cadence feels off."

"I'm working on it!" Dr. Simon barked. "Speaking of cuddly . . ." His eyes darted around the van. "Where's Merle?"

"Escaped," Delilah announced as she approached from the animal transporter she had driven from Old Town Nazareth, filled with the talking animals in her charge there.

"Escaped?!!! How could that be?!!!" Dr. Simon jabbed a finger at Ruben.

"You had one job, Ruben! One job!!!"
he shrieked.

"We re-captured Pearl . . ." Ruben
weakly offered.

"Where is she?" Dr. Simon looked
back into the van.

"She re-re-escaped," Delilah said
coolly, only too happy to lay the blame
for Pearl's getaway on Ruben.

"This is unacceptable! UNACCEPT-
ABLE!!!" Dr. Simon blared. "The park
opens in a few days, and I must have
those squirrels!!!" Since learning of the
existence of Merle and Pearl, two talking squirrels from the first century,
Dr. Simon had made the Dead Sea
Squirrels the centerpiece of BabbleLand.
With the Passover and Easter holidays
close at hand and the associated surge

of tourists to Jerusalem, he had been counting on having the important historical and cuddly rodent relics as the main attraction needed to make opening day a success.

"Sir, if I may?" Delilah cunningly offered. "I did manage to capture two talking donkeys—descendants

of Balaam's donkey. An unexpected bonus."

"At least there's one person I can count on!" Dr. Simon replied. "Ruben—you are off squirrel duty! You are being demoted to Gomez babysitter."

"I don't need a babysitter!" Michael protested.

"And why is that a demotion?" Dr. Gomez wondered.

"I don't know if you guys know this, but I'm not a Gomez," Justin said.

"Me neither," Sadie added.

"Do not take your eyes off these six humans, whatever their last names are, until Delilah and I can re-re-re-capture those squirrels! Got it?!" Dr. Simon ordered Ruben.

"Yes sir," Ruben replied pitifully.

CHAPTER 3

Anything but another date!

Merle complained, standing beneath a palm tree. He and Dave had been scouring the riverbank for squirrel-worthy food for the last hour.

"Look," Dave reasoned, "I can eat bugs. So could you, by the way, if you had the stomach for it."

"I don't," Merle confirmed.

"And Adriana can eat grass. I'm just saying, if you and Pearl want to eat . . ." Dave began as he pointed up toward the fronds of the tree. The day before, Merle and Dave had completely gorged themselves on dates, the super-sweet fruit of the date palm tree. If you have ever eaten so much of something that it made you sick, you'll understand why Merle never cared to see another date in his life.

"Uuugh . . ." Merle sighed. "You're right." He began to climb the tree. He figured Pearl would enjoy a date or two for breakfast, and they would at least keep him from starving to death.

"Pssst." A whisper drifted from a tree nearby.

"Did you say something?" Merle asked, looking back over his shoulder.

"Wasn't me," Dave answered.

"Chessstnutsss are tasssty . . ." the voice said.

"Who's there?!!!" Merle asked, climbing back down the palm.

"Up here . . . In thisss chessstnut tree . . ."

"Chestnuts? I love chestnuts!" Merle looked up toward a scraggly cypress. "Is that a chestnut tree?" he wondered.

Dave returned a shrug, having no reason as a lizard to be familiar with tree species.

"Oh yesss . . . Tasssty chessstnutsss."

"Wow. I had no idea they grew this far south!" Merle said cheerfully as he headed toward the tree. "Thanks for the tip, buddy!"

"Merle, I don't know if it's a good idea . . ." Dave watched suspiciously as Merle scampered up into the cypress.

Merle puffed like getting punched in the gut, now suddenly coiled in the clutches of a huge snake!

CHAPTER 4

"Where are you taking us, Ruben?!"
Dr. Gomez demanded as the church
van wound its way through the narrow
streets of Jerusalem.

"Usually that's not a question a kid-
napper is required to answer," Ruben
replied. "Did you tell *me* where we
were going when I was the kidnapped
one?"

"As a matter of fact, we did," Mrs.
Gomez said. "Where we were going
was the subject of every conversation."

"Well, I never asked," Ruben
grumbled. "I can't believe I've been
demoted to shuttle driver. This is so
humiliating."

"Dr. Simon is pretty good at humiliating you," Michael called out from
the back. "Why do you keep following
his orders? Why don't you just tell him
to forget it and get another job?"

The question, while being a very
practical one, seemed to confuse Ruben.
"I . . . Um . . . I . . . It's my job. I am a
highly trained agent of espionage," he
stammered.

"And a shuttle driver," Justin added.

"I've put so much work into finding
those squirrels!" Ruben fumed, pound-
ing his fist on the steering wheel and
sounding the horn. "I followed you all
the way to Tennessee. I devised a brilliant scheme to capture them using
drones. Brought them back to Israel.
Lost them, chased them, found them,
lost them. I can't quit now."

"Sure you can," Sadie said calmly.

"What are you talking about?!" Ruben barked.

"Sunk cost fallacy," Sadie replied, matter-of-factly.

"My question remains, *What are you talking about?*" Ruben repeated.

"Look." Sadie leaned forward. "You're focused on how much work you've put into capturing the squirrels instead of the benefits you could have right now and in the future if you just stopped chasing after them."

"Smart girl . . ." Mrs. Gomez whispered to her husband.

"Yes . . . I was considering the same argument," Dr. Gomez replied quietly.

"Sure you were, dear," Mrs. Gomez said, patting her husband's shoulder.

"What kind of benefits?" Ruben barked.

"Like not being miserable and getting a chance to take a shower," Justin quipped as he waved his hand under his nose. "I'm just saying."

"Do you really think Dr. Simon is going to pay you for all the work you've done? Even *if* he's able to find the squirrels?" Michael asked.

"Stop confusing me!" Ruben demanded. "Did I confuse *you* when I was the kidnapped one?!"

CHAPTER 5

"You didn't tell me you were a snake!" Merle grunted under the tightening loops of the serpent.

"Oopsss . . . Sssorry, mussst have ssslipped my mind," hissed the snake.

"And what about the chestnuts?!"

"Sssilly sssquirrel, there are no chessstnutsss. It'sss a cccypresss."

"Well, that was a flat-out lie, wasn't it then?" Merle protested in offense.

"I'm a sssnake. What did you exsssspect?"

"Wait a second!" Dave pleaded from below. "You speak human! *We* speak human!" The lizard opened his arms wide in solidarity. "From one rare

talking reptile to another, what do you
say you give the rare talking mammal
a break?"

"Yeah. Gimme a break . . . Just not
my ribs," Merle begged, nearly breath-
less. "Plus, it's not just us. We need to
rescue a family and a whole zooful
of talking animals!"

"Ssso sssorry, a sssnake'sss gotta eat,"
the serpent said. That much was true.
Regardless of a prey's language skills,
the desert is a harsh environment, and
a predator cannot afford to pass up a
meal. Plus, there's no getting around
the fact that snakes are always the
bad guys.

"Help!!!" Dave yelled out desper-
ately. But surely there was no way
Adriana and Pearl could hear him—
they were too far away and dead

asleep! *Could I pry Merle loose myself?*
Dave wondered. *Not a chance, snakes
are too muscular,* he reasoned. He'd
only succeed in getting eaten along
with Merle. That's when he saw it—
a feather at the base of the tree, no
doubt left over from a bird of a previous meal.

"I can't believe you lied to me,"
Merle moaned. "I love chestnuts."

"And sssquirrelsss are ssscrump-
tiousss . . ." the snake hissed, coming
eye to eye with Merle and tightening
his grip.

"Hrgr . . ." Merle grunted.

"Huh?" the snake said as he felt something on his belly. He turned to find Dave holding a feather. "What are you doing?" he asked coldly.

"I'm . . . tickling you . . . ?" Dave offered timidly.

"No, you are not. Sssnakes are not tick . . . AHHHHH!" Suddenly, the snake uncoiled faster than a yo-yo, dropping Merle as he was yanked off the branch, his tail now in the grip of Adriana's teeth! As Merle fell safely to the ground, the alpaca stood with her forelegs on the trunk of the tree, wildly shaking the snake back and forth like a pool noodle. "WHAAAA!!!!! SSSSSSSTOPPPPP!" the serpent screamed.

"Hmm . . ." Adriana hummed— alpaca for "Not yet." She then pushed away from the tree and with all four hooves on the ground swung the snake in circles like an Olympic hammer thrower. When you have a long neck like an alpaca, you can generate impressive centrifugal force.

LET GOOOOO!

the snake dizzily pleaded.

"Hmm," Adriana replied, which is

alpaca for "Okay." She released her
bite on the snake's tail, which sent him
sailing high through the air, scream-
ing as he flew over the Jordan and into
the bulrushes on the opposite shore.

"Whoa." Slack-jawed, Merle and
Dave marveled in unison.

CHAPTER 6

Mmmm! Delicious!

Pearl declared, licking date goo from her paws under their leafy hideout. "Are you sure you don't want one, Merle?"

"Erp," Merle burped, feeling nauseous at the idea of eating another sweet gooey date ever again. "I had my heart set on chestnuts."

"There were never any chestnuts, my friend," Dave said from his roost on a branch above. "You're just lucky to be alive. Who knew alpacas are such light sleepers?" He gave Adriana a pat. "And have such great hearing! Good girl!"

"Hmm . . ." Adriana hummed.

"Yes! Absolutely!" Merle said. "I can't thank you enough, Adriana. Being swallowed whole by a snake is not the way I want to go." Merle turned to Dave. "You really thought tickling would work?"

"I was under a lot of pressure." Dave shrugged. "I did what I could."

After a day of rest, the group resumed their mission at sunset, traveling south along the river. Merle took Pearl's advice and sat next to her on Adriana's withers, which made for a much smoother ride. Without Adriana, the trip would have taken them nearly a

week, but alpacas can run as fast as
35 miles per hour, so they made it to
Jericho in just one night!

At sunset the next night they struck
out on the Old Jericho Road toward
Jerusalem.
   "Help! I twisted my ankle
and can't walk!" a familiar-
looking hiker called out
from a boulder along the
trail, holding his foot.
"Will you be a good Sam—"
   "You again?!"
Merle interrupted.
"We fell for this
act once already."

"Hey! You're the birdcage squirrels," the hiker said. "I didn't know you could talk!"

"Well enough to tell you to stop scamming kindhearted tourists," Pearl chided.

"Yeah, well, look, could you be a Good Samaritan and not tell any-one?"

"That's not how that works," Pearl remarked. "Why don't you just stop being a *Scamaritan*?"

"Good one, Pearly!" Merle remarked, impressed by Pearl's play on words. "Want some dates?" Merle tossed the hiker a few fruits on their way by.

"Thanks, buddy!" the Scamaritan replied.

CHAPTER 7

"Please tell me you have a plan for finding Merle and Pearl." Dr. Simon grilled Delilah as the two walked through BabbleLand that evening. Workers scurried about, putting the finishing touches onto park attractions, including the Red Sea Rapids, the Goliath Coaster, and the Chariots of Fire Ferris Wheel—along with numerous animal enclosures.

"You'll never find them!" Dusty  called out from his Moab Mountain paddock.

"You tell 'em, Uncle Dusty!" his nephew Ham chimed in.

"Quiet, donkeys!" Dr. Simon barked.

"This is the downside of being surrounded by talking animals," he
grumbled.

"I'm working on it, sir," Delilah
answered nervously. "I'm in commu-
nication with our contacts all over the
country. It's only a matter of time."

"Hmmm. We'll see about that," Dr.
Simon grunted as they passed the Eden
enclosure. "I certainly hope you prove
more productive than Ruben."

"Psst . . ." a quiet voice whispered.

Dr. Simon swiveled toward Delilah.
"Did you say something?"

"No sir," Delilah replied.

"Sssome sssquirrel newsss?" the
s-loving voice said.

Dr. Simon and Delilah turned to see
a snake resting on a low branch of a
fruit tree in the center of the garden.

AHHH!

Delilah startled and took a few steps back. "I don't like snakes!"

"I don't like you either," the snake said, "but you might like what I have to sssay . . ."

"What have you heard, Scarlett?!" the doctor asked the snake eagerly, clutching the bars of the enclosure.

"Your friendsss are on their way. Two sssquirrels, a liss-sard, and a very aggresssssive alpaca," Scarlett replied.

"Where did you hear this?" Delilah wondered.

"My sssisssster'sss sssson."

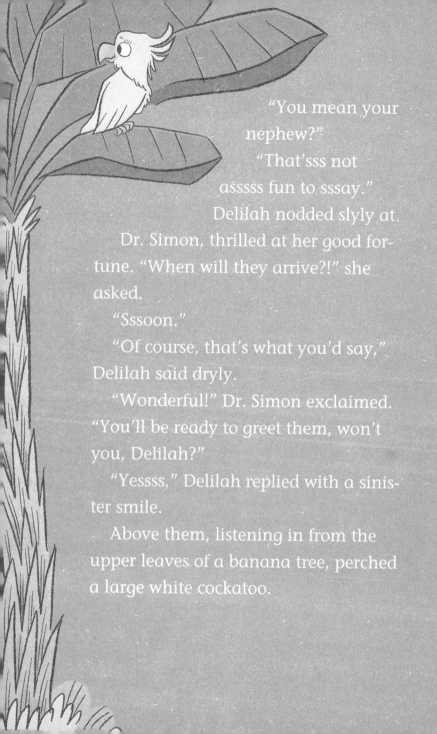

"You mean your
nephew?"

"That'sss not
asssss fun to sssay."

Delilah nodded slyly at
Dr. Simon, thrilled at her good for-
tune. "When will they arrive?!" she
asked.

"Sssoon."

"Of course, that's what you'd say,"
Delilah said dryly.

"Wonderful!" Dr. Simon exclaimed.
"You'll be ready to greet them, won't
you, Delilah?"

"Yessss," Delilah replied with a sinis-
ter smile.

Above them, listening in from the
upper leaves of a banana tree, perched
a large white cockatoo.

CHAPTER 8

It turns out that three small animals riding on the back of an alpaca take quite a while longer to get through a city than the open countryside—even in the middle of the night. The uphill climb along the Old Jericho Road took only a few hours, but once Adriana, Merle, Pearl, and Dave reached the eastern edge of Jerusalem, the going became much slower. Dodging traffic and avoiding being noticed by people turned what could have been a one-hour walk into a seven-hour sneak. By the time they arrived at the BabbleLand site on the southwestern side of the city, it was well into the morning.

"There it is," Pearl announced as they approached the park, which looked much more finished than the last time she had seen it, with its cable cars and roller coaster tracks towering high above.

"Impressive," Dave marveled.

"Maybe we can go on some rides after we rescue the Gomezes?" Merle wondered, starting toward the fence.

"Don't get distracted," Pearl answered, pulling him back.

"Maybe we could just watch a parade?"

"Merle and Pearl!" A voice rang out from above. Before the squirrels could look up, a large white cockatoo landed in front of Adriana. "Follow me," the bird said and disappeared into a thicket of bushes.

"Do we know you?" Merle asked as they followed her in.

"I'm Debbie. A Zephaniah's cockatoo," she whispered. "We are being watched and we don't have much time. Delilah knows you are coming, so you mustn't enter the park."

"How would she know that?" Pearl asked.

"Any run-in with snakes lately?"
Debbie asked.

Hmm...

Adriana confirmed.
Pearl looked
worried. "What
about the Gomezes?"

"Oh, they're not here," Debbie said. "They're in the Christian Quarter of the Old City." She pointed northeast with her wing. The Old City of Jerusalem (also called the Fortress of Zion and the City of David) is surrounded by ancient walls and divided into four sections: the Armenian Quarter, the Christian Quarter, the Muslim Quarter, and the Jewish Quarter.

"We just passed the Old City on our way here," Dave noted.

"How do we get to them?" Pearl pleaded.

"Enter the city by the Zion Gate," Debbie said. "Pass through the Armenian Quarter, following the signs for the Church of the Holy Sepulchre.

I'll meet you there and give you further instructions."

"Got it," Dave said.

"Why can't you just tell us now?" Pearl wondered.

"No time!" Debbie said and flew away.

CHAPTER 9

"Bad bird!" Delilah sneered at the monitor wall inside the state-of-the-art BabbleLand security control center. She had seen Adriana, the squirrels, and Dave follow a cockatoo into the bushes and was now watching the alpaca run northeast. Realizing they had been tipped off, Delilah reached for her

phone. "I need you at the Zion Gate immediately. Be on the lookout for an alpaca carrying two squirrels and a lizard." She quickly took the phone away from her ear as the loud sound of laughter rang through. "Yes, I'm being serious. I will meet you there!" she said as she grabbed her car keys off the desk.

It was difficult enough sneaking through the outskirts of Jerusalem during the night and early morning without being seen; doing it during broad daylight was an entirely different matter. After multiple dives behind park benches, through alleyways, and into a dumpster or two, Merle, Pearl, Dave, and Adriana

arrived outside the Zion Gate by midafternoon. If you're wondering why it's called the Zion Gate, it's because it leads to Mount Zion and is a passageway through the 40-foot-tall stone wall that surrounds the Old City. Coming from the southwest, it's the quickest way into the Old City and the straightest path to the Church of the Holy Sepulchre, which is why it was the perfect place for Delilah and her henchmen to lie in wait.

"Uh-oh!" Pearl gasped as Adriana rounded a corner with her riders. Delilah stood with two large men blocking the entrance of the gate about 100 yards ahead. Immediately, Adriana ducked into the nearest doorway. The animals found themselves in an old building at the foot of a set of stairs.

"Do you think they saw us?" Merle wondered as they climbed the stairs.

"Pretty sure no," Pearl said.

"What is this place?" Dave marveled as they exited the stairway into a large hall on the second floor. Sweeping stone arches towered above them.

"The Cenacle," Merle read from a plaque on the wall. "A hall built in the Middle Ages at the place where, according to Christian tradition, Jesus ate the Passover meal with his disciples, just before the crucifixion."

"The Last Supper," Pearl realized.

"Supper . . ." Merle repeated dreamily, having eaten only dates for the last two days. "I sure could go for some chicken nuggets."

"Focus, Merle," Pearl directed.

CHAPTER 10

"What's the Last Supper?" Dave asked. Having spent most of his life in Bethany Beyond the Jordan, the lizard knew the story of Jesus' baptism—he had heard it from tour guides a million times—but he had never heard this part of Jesus' story.

"Matthew, Mark, Luke, and John wrote about it in their records," Pearl explained. "So did Paul in his first letter to the Corinthians."

The animals had settled in an alcove below a window to rest. Adriana's head, atop her long neck, stuck up high enough for her to see outside and keep watch.

Pearl continued, "The Last Supper happened when Jesus had come to Jerusalem with his disciples for the next part of God's plan. By the time he arrived, he was very well known all over the country and the people here welcomed him as a king, shouting,

This made the people in charge very nervous. They didn't want to give up their power to a new king, so they made their own plan to get rid of Jesus. But they couldn't outsmart God—because their plan was actually *part* of God's plan!"

"God's clever like that," Merle said.

"I'm not following you," Dave admitted, scratching his back against a stone column. "What exactly *was* God's plan?"

"Jesus knew that he would soon die," Pearl replied.

"Wait. Dying was part of the plan?"

"It was," Pearl said. "Jesus gathered with his disciples here in this room. Before they ate, Jesus washed their feet because he wanted them to know the reason that he had come to earth was to serve people and give his life for them. He wanted them to always remember what he was about to do. Then, as they all gathered around the table for supper, Jesus held up a loaf of bread and thanked God for it."

"A loaf of bread . . ." Merle interrupted wistfully, clutching his grumbling stomach. "I bet it was warm and soft."

"Then he said," Pearl continued, choosing to remain in the moment, "'This is my body that is broken for you. Take and eat. Every time you do, remember me.' He then held up a cup of wine and thanked God for it and said, 'This is my blood that will be poured out to forgive the sins of many. Take and drink. Every time you do, remember me.'"

"The bread and wine help us to remember that Jesus died so people could be forgiven?" Dave asked.

"Exactly!" Pearl replied. "And how much he loved us."

"Hmm," Adriana added.

"An alpaca amen!" Merle said.

CHAPTER 11

"Hmm . . ." Adriana hummed again.

"Yes. Praise the Lord. Looks like she's having a moment here, guys." Merle smiled.

"Hmm . . ."

"Look!" Pearl squeaked, following Adriana's gaze through an open window. While Adriana might have understood and enjoyed Pearl's story, her hums were actually directed at a sight across the street. A dress form stood visible through a second-floor window just across the alley from them. And on the dress form hung a wedding dress. "You think that will work, girl?" Pearl asked with a gasp.

"Hmm . . ." Adriana nodded.

"Hmm?" Adriana asked, now robed in a bridal gown and veil.

"You look . . . lovely, dear," Pearl noted tentatively.

After the group had snuck back across the alleyway, careful to avoid being spotted by the crew setting up for an evening wedding, they had located the bridal dressing room in the building across from the Cenacle.

Have you ever dressed your dog up to look like a lion or a dinosaur? It's super cute. But *cute* might not be the word you would use to describe an alpaca dressed up like a bride. In truth, Adriana simply looked like an alpaca in a wedding dress.

"Maybe this will help?" Pearl added, grabbing a tube of red lipstick from a makeup tray and applying it to her friend's black lips. Next, she grabbed some mascara and brushed it on Adriana's eyelashes.

"They grow up so fast." Merle sniffed and wiped away a tear before offering Adriana a long white veil to complete her ensemble.

"Is she supposed to be on four legs?" Dave wondered.

"No. Humans only have two legs," Pearl conceded, frowning.

"I have an idea!" Merle said.

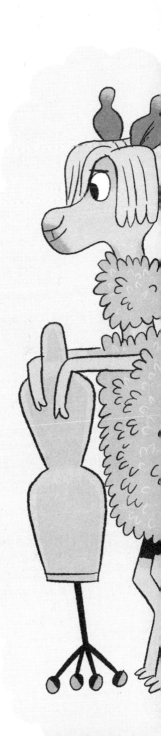

CHAPTER 12

Under the warm light of the late after-
noon sun, an extremely tall and
long-necked bride shuffled awkwardly
through the streets of Jerusalem.

Clomp . . . Clomp . . . Clomp . . .
Adriana's rear hooves sounded off the
cobblestones.

"Shhh! Step lighter!" Merle whispered from under the wedding gown.
Concealed beneath its flowing skirt, he,
Pearl, and Dave followed the wheeled
dress form that Adriana was using to
keep balance on her hind legs.

"Hmm . . ." Adriana replied quietly,
which means in alpaca, "I'm trying!"

An alpaca is tall enough when

standing on all fours. Their necks are the length of their legs, and their heads stand about shoulder height to most adult humans. But upright on her hind legs, she was as tall as a professional basketball player. Fortunately, her semi-transparent veil covered her fuzzy neck and concealed most of her face (other than her bright-red lips and deep black eyelashes).

"Are we headed toward the gate?" Merle whispered.

"Hmm . . ." Adriana confirmed. Soon, the four found themselves surrounded by a group of tourists also headed into the Old City through the Zion Gate. Compliments came drifting from the crowd.

"Congratulations," a man said.

"You look stunning," a woman commented.

"*Stun* is a good word," Merle whispered.

"Shhh," Pearl shushed.

Adriana tried not to look directly at Delilah and her two henchmen standing watch at the gate. But out of the corner of her eye, she noticed one of the men staring at her. As she passed, she turned his way, batted her eyelashes, and shot him an air kiss. Shocked, the henchman blushed and diverted his eyes.

"Guys! I think we're through," Dave exclaimed. He was right, they had made it safely through the gate and were now in the Armenian Quarter of the Old City. Adriana pushed away the dress form and fell back to all fours.

"Let's find that church!" Pearl said.

CHAPTER 13

This way!

Merle said, pointing at a sign that read "Church of the Holy Sepulchre."

Everyone climbed on Adriana's back and they moved down the crowded, narrow street. Tourists and locals pressed around them as they passed under carved archways, by shops and ancient homes, some nearly as old as Merle and Pearl.

"Look, Momma, a camel bride!"

61

a small boy said, dragging at his mom's arm.

"Ya, baby, that's—um—normal here," the harried mom improvised.

Soon they found themselves in a covered alleyway market packed with vendors and tourists. T-shirts, purses, scarves, dresses, and shoes spilled out of small shops to their left; bracelets, souvenirs, postcards, and candles packed bazaars to their right.

"How much for the camel wedding dress?" one man shouted.

"What are you talking about?!" a shop owner answered as Adriana wound her way through the crowd. Suddenly, the sky opened up above them again.

"This is the Christian Quarter! I think we're close!" Dave whispered, pointing out a number of souvenir crosses and paintings of Jesus in the shops around them. Dave was right. No sooner had he said the words than they came to an arched entryway under a sign that read, "Holy Sepulchre." The friends passed through into the courtyard of the ancient church, its stone walls towering over them.

"Whoa." Dave gasped at the impressive sight.

"Where's the bird?" Merle wondered, looking around the nearly deserted courtyard for Debbie. "Did she say *by* the church or *in* the church?"

"I don't know that she specified," Pearl answered.

"Well, we can't stand out here for long. We're sitting ducks if Delilah shows up," Merle said.

"I'm not a duck," Dave noted.

"It's a saying," Merle clarified.

"I say we get inside while we still can," Pearl said, and they ducked into the church. (It's a saying).

CHAPTER 14

SQUIRREL'S-EYE VIEW

"Welcome to the church of the Holy Sepulchre," a guide announced to a small group assembled for the last tour of the evening.

"Oooh! Let's join 'em!" Merle whispered enthusiastically. "I love these!"

"Merle—we have to keep out of sight and watch for Debbie," Pearl cautioned.

"We will," Merle promised as they hid behind a pillar.

"*Sepulchre* means a small room cut in rock in which a dead person is laid," the guide continued. "This church is built on the site of the crucifixion, burial, and resurrection of Jesus. It's

one of the oldest churches in the world;
originally built in the year AD 335, five
years after the Church of the Nativity."

"I remember that one," Pearl said,
recalling the place she and Merle had
narrowly escaped Ruben. She'd been
dressed as an angelic squirrel at the
time. They followed the tour up a stair-
case under an arch marked *Golgotha*.

"After the Last Supper," the guide
continued, "Jesus was brought before
the religious and political leaders in
Jerusalem. They did not understand
the Good News that Jesus brought
about the Kingdom of God. They were
angry and afraid that Jesus was caus-
ing too much trouble for them and
their own kingdom, so the Roman
governor Pilate sentenced Jesus to
death. On Good Friday, they brought

Jesus here to Golgotha, which means 'the place of the skull.'"

The guide paused under a mosaic of Jesus being nailed to a cross. "Roman soldiers attached him to a cross by driving nails into his hands and feet. Then they pushed up the cross and waited for Jesus to die. Jesus hung on the cross for many hours."

"That must have been very painful for him," Pearl whispered with tears in her eyes.

"Jesus could have called an army of angels to save him, but he knew this was God's plan—to give his life to rescue us—so that we could live with God forever." The guide continued to an altar in front of a statue of Jesus hanging on the cross. "Finally, when the land was covered in darkness, he died."

CHAPTER 15

SQUIRREL'S-EYE
VIEW

Adriana, Merle, Pearl, and Dave followed the tour group down another set of stairs and through a long marble hall.

"Step softly, girl," Pearl whispered to Adriana as they passed into a large rotunda, or domed circular room, full of echoes.

"Jesus' followers wrapped his body in clean cloths and placed him in a tomb cut out of rock," the guide announced as the group gathered around a large ornate stone structure in the middle of the room.

"A sepulchre," Merle repeated proudly.

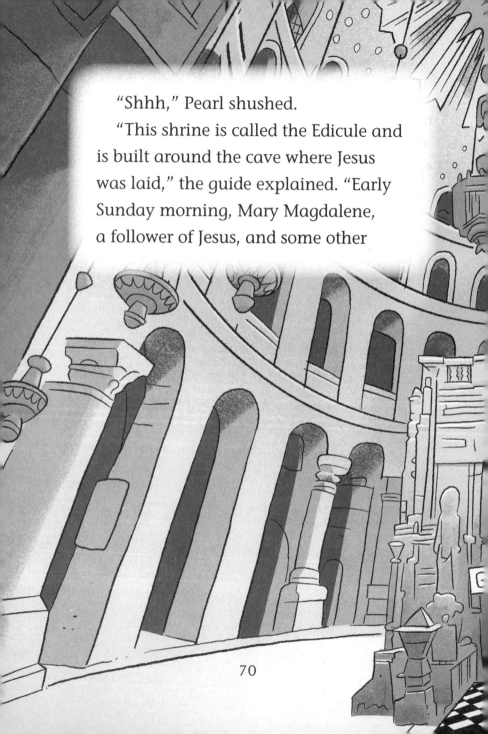

"Shhh," Pearl shushed.

"This shrine is called the Edicule and is built around the cave where Jesus was laid," the guide explained. "Early Sunday morning, Mary Magdalene, a follower of Jesus, and some other

70

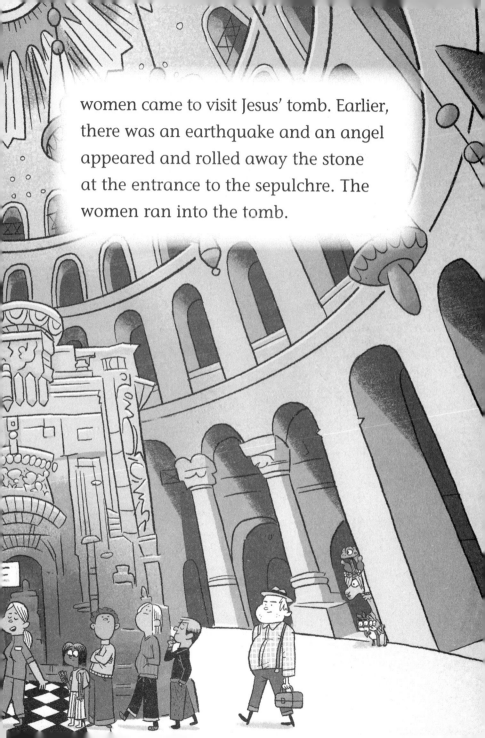

women came to visit Jesus' tomb. Earlier, there was an earthquake and an angel appeared and rolled away the stone at the entrance to the sepulchre. The women ran into the tomb.

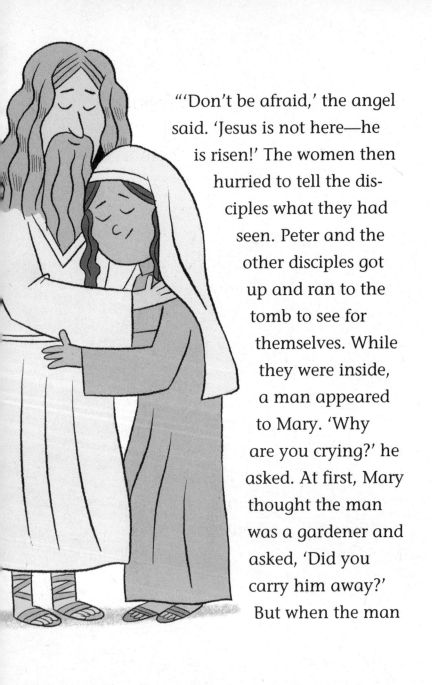

"'Don't be afraid,' the angel said. 'Jesus is not here—he is risen!' The women then hurried to tell the disciples what they had seen. Peter and the other disciples got up and ran to the tomb to see for themselves. While they were inside, a man appeared to Mary. 'Why are you crying?' he asked. At first, Mary thought the man was a gardener and asked, 'Did you carry him away?' But when the man said her name, 'Mary,' she knew right away that it was Jesus!"

"Hmm!" Adriana happily hummed, her voice echoing around the rotunda.

"Yes. Mary must have been very glad," the guide replied. "Later that night, when Peter and most of the other disciples were gathered in the same room where they had eaten the Last Supper, Jesus appeared to them. 'Peace be with you!' Jesus said and showed them the marks in his hands and side. It was really him. Jesus had risen from the dead—just like he said! He had defeated death so that we could live with him forever!"

"His rescue mission was complete!" Merle whispered.

CHAPTER 16

"There you are!" Debbie's voice rang out behind them. Adriana, Merle, Pearl, and Dave turned to see the cockatoo perched on a pillar above. "Sorry I'm late."

"That's okay, we had time for a lovely tour," Pearl replied.

"What's with the dress?" Debbie asked, looking at Adriana.

"We had to sneak past Delilah at the Zion Gate—somehow she knew we'd be there," Merle said.

Debbie nodded. "She's got eyes everywhere. Way to improvise. And Adriana—you're stunning."

"Hmm . . ." Adriana replied, fluttering her eyelashes.

"Follow me," Debbie said. She swooped down and out the door of the church and into the night.

Debbie led the alpaca, squirrels, and lizard through the narrow streets and covered alleyways. In just a few minutes they reached the entrance of a hostel—which is like a hotel but much less fancy. Like every building in the Old City, it not only looked like it had been there over a thousand years, but it actually had. The front door was cracked open.

"This is it," the cockatoo said.

They hurried past Debbie through the door into the small empty lobby. A few old chairs and sofas were pushed up against the rough stone walls and a check-in desk sat unattended.

"Debbie, where is . . ." Pearl began before the sound of the front door closing cut off her question. To their horror, they turned to see . . .

Ruben standing by the now-shut door—with Debbie perched on his shoulder.

Merle and Pearl screamed, horrified.

"Who's this guy?" Dave asked, less
horrified.

"Ruben!" Merle answered.

"Like the sandwich?" Dave
wondered.

"We've been tricked!" Pearl
lamented.

Adriana snarled, ready to charge at
Ruben.

"Wait! Wait! It's all good! You have
not been tricked!" Ruben assured them,
holding his palms out toward the pro-
tective alpaca. "You look stunning, by
the way."

"Merle! Pearl!" another voice called
from behind them. They turned to
see . . .

Michael standing with his mom,
dad, sister, Justin, and Sadie.

Merle and Pearl screamed again.

"Who are they?" Dave asked, not sure if he should be horrified or not.

"Our friends!" Merle answered as he and Pearl hopped off Adriana and ran to the Gomezes.

"That's . . . good?" Dave asked as Merle hugged Michael's leg, Sadie scooped up Pearl, and Justin gave Adriana an awkward hug. "Yes. It seems to be good," Dave surmised.

"I'm super confused," Merle admitted.

"Ruben's helping us," Michael said.

Pearl turned to Ruben. "Wait, what?!"

"Michael is right," Ruben said. "I arranged to have Debbie warn you to steer clear of BabbleLand and lead you here, where I've been hiding the Gomezes."

"He's nice now!" Jane cheered.

"Why didn't you tell us, Debbie?" Pearl asked.

"He told me you wouldn't believe it," Debbie said.

"Yeah, you were probably right about that," replied Merle.

Ruben gestured toward the door. "I have the van waiting to drive you all to Tel Aviv airport. There is still time to catch a flight tonight."

"We picked these up for you!" Mrs. Gomez said cheerfully as she dangled two tiny emotional support vests for the squirrels.

"We're going home!" Dr. Gomez announced.

"Woo-hoo!" the kids cheered.

"Hold on! We're not going anywhere," Merle proclaimed. "We have another friend to rescue!"

CHAPTER 17

"Did you switch perfumes, dear?" the mother of the bride asked as she helped her daughter on with her wedding gown. "I like it. Earthy, yet floral."

That was actually a pretty decent description for the scent combination of alpaca and lavender deodorizer. Thankful for the temporary use of Adriana's disguise, Pearl thought it important to return the dress on their way out of the Old City so as not to ruin the bride-to-be's special day. And Mrs. Gomez thought it important to de-alpaca it with her stash of Febreze.

"It's not safe to go back to BabbleLand," Dr. Gomez worried from the front passenger seat as Ruben drove the van back toward the park.

"We can't abandon Dusty," Merle pleaded from the second row. "If it wasn't for him, who knows if we would have ever found each other?"

"You're right," Dr. Gomez conceded. "But how are we going to get him out?"

"I've got some thoughts," Ruben said.

"Why did you decide all of a sudden to help us?" Merle asked from the back row between Justin and Sadie.

"I've had it with Dr. Simon," Ruben confessed.

"A real cost sinker," Sadie added.

"Besides, I've grown to like your family and Pearl."

"What about me?!" Merle asked.

"Maybe you'll grow on me one day," Ruben said.

"Thanks . . . buddy?" Merle replied.

Ruben turned off the headlights as they rolled onto the BabbleLand grounds and pulled the van into an unlit maintenance entrance. "I've made sure this gate is unlocked," he announced as the van came to a stop. "Do you know where to find him?"

"Moab Mountain?" Sadie said.

"Smart girl," Ruben replied. East of the Dead Sea and in modern-day Jordan, Moab was the land where the story of Balaam's donkey took place in the Bible.

"Where will you be?" Dr. Gomez asked Ruben as the group piled quietly out of the van.

"Don't worry about me. Just get Dusty and meet me back here," Ruben replied.

With Dr. Gomez's (and Sadie's) knowledge of Holy Land geography, it didn't take long to find the Moab Mountain paddock—even in the dark.

"Dusty?" Merle whispered as the group approached the pen.

"Merle? Is that you?" Dusty answered as he popped up from the bed of straw where he was lying.

"I'm here too!" Ham added.

"We've come to rescue you!" Merle announced as Michael and Justin moved toward the gate to the enclosure.

"Oh, have you now?" a man's voice rang out as a bank of lights burst on, lighting up the area like midday. It was Dr. Simon, flanked by Delilah and several strong henchmen with lassos and nets!

CHAPTER 18

"Congratulations on your superb work, Delilah!" Dr. Simon told his new favorite accomplice.

"Yes. The squirrels have delivered themselves." Delilah beamed proudly. "Just as planned." She tapped her fingers together like the true villain she was. With the donkey paddock behind the Gomezes and a line of baddies in front, the friends had no hope of escape.

"We're sitting ducks!" Merle lamented.

"What's with you and ducks?" Dave wondered.

"Oh my! This just keeps getting

better!" Dr. Simon squealed with glee.
"A Lizard of Judah! This is more awe-
some than I ever could have imagined!
I've searched high and low for you,
and now you came to me, you beauti-
ful blue tourist magnet!"

"Why . . . thank you?" Dave replied.

"Delilah, you are SOOOOO much
smarter than Ruben!" Dr. Simon
beamed.

"Is that so?" Ruben mumbled under his breath from inside BabbleLand's vacant security center in another area of the park, watching and listening over a large wall of monitors. The guards who would have normally been there were currently surrounding the Gomezes.

"Are you going to put us in cages too?" Michael asked.

"Yes! Exactly!" Dr. Simon replied. "You'll be going to jail for breaking and entering."

"And attempted grand theft donkey!" Delilah added.

"You're the one who stole us, Delilah," Dusty said.

Justin scratched his head. "Is grand theft donkey an actual thing?"

"Generally, theft of property over $500 is considered grand theft," Sadie said.

"Each or together?" Ham muttered to Dusty.

"How does she know these things?" Mrs. Gomez wondered.

Dr. Gomez shrugged. "Beats me."

"I told you, Sadie knows every-thing," Michael said.

"Not everything," Sadie admitted. "Like . . . for instance, I have no idea how we're going to escape."

"I do." Ruben smiled slyly from behind the security control panel, his right index finger hovering above the *ALL UNLOCK* button.

"That's enough out of all of you!" Dr. Simon barked. "There'll be no trouble

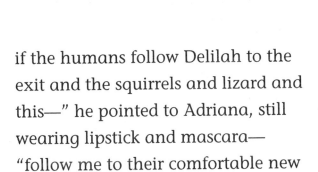

if the humans follow Delilah to the exit and the squirrels and lizard and this—" he pointed to Adriana, still wearing lipstick and mascara— "follow me to their comfortable new homes."

"This isn't our home!" Pearl protested.

"We'll see about that!" Dr. Simon yelled as his guards advanced with outstretched nets.

Then Ruben pushed the button.

CHAPTER 19

BUZZZZZ!

Loudspeakers sounded as all the lights
in the whole park switched on. Then
all at once, every door to every cage,
enclosure, entry, and exit gate in
BabbleLand sprang open!

"AHHHH!" Dr. Simon and Delilah
screamed in unison. Can you imag-
ine trying to stop a leak in a rowboat
where 100 holes open up all at once?
You wouldn't have enough fingers or
toes to stop the water from pouring
in! Four guards with nets could easily
grab two squirrels and a lizard, but
it was impossible for them to handle
the stream of talking beasts suddenly

making a break for the exits. It was like all the animals somehow exited from Noah's ark at once—and not in a neat and orderly manner.

"Yeah, boy!" bellowed a galloping camel in a deep voice as it bolted from the Withered Wilderness enclosure.

"Yippee!" An adolescent antelope ran after.

"Mama—I'm comin' home!" a tiny tortoise squeaked as she slowly crawled toward the exit. Cheering animal voices could be heard erupting from all over the park.

Overwhelmed, the open-mouthed guards simply looked around help-lessly.

"Fly, you fools!" Debbie the cocka-too called down to the Gomezes as she flew by. She circled back immediately. "Sorry! You can't fly and you're not fools! It's a saying!"

"Run!" Michael shouted, and they all scattered. Dr. and Mrs. Gomez ran with Jane in one direction; Michael, Justin, and Sadie in another; Dusty and Ham in a third; Merle, Pearl, and Dave in a fourth; and Adriana in a fifth.

"Get them!!!" Dr. Simon shouted at the guards.

"Get who?" one guard asked, confused.

"The squirrels!" yelled Dr. Simon, realizing that years of planning and hard work were now going down the drain. He could not bear to let his most prized attractions slip away.

RED SEA

"Where to?!" Dave hollered.

"Away from them!" Merle answered, looking over his shoulder at four guards in hot pursuit.

"There!" Pearl shouted, pointing to one of the park's water rides called Red Sea Rapids.

Ruben, from his view in the control center, activated the attraction, and water immediately began to flow. A hollow log released from the log corral

and paused at the start gate. The
squirrels and Dave jumped in. Ruben
released them on their way.

"We're off!" Merle shouted.

"Yes, but I'm afraid we'll end up right
back at the start," Pearl said as she
noted the direction of the ride flumes.
"It's just a big loop!" Thankfully, the
pursuing guards were not as perceptive
as Pearl. They didn't think twice about
jumping into a second log released by
Ruben.

"You'll never catch us!" Merle yelled back confidently to the guards as the squirrels' log gathered speed. *CLUNK!* Suddenly they came to a stop and the nose of their log tilted upward. Now the guards' log was gaining fast. "What's happening?!" Merle wondered as they clicked slowly up into the sky.

"We're going up!" Dave answered. "Way up!"

Merle spun forward to see that they were climbing an enormous track. Have you ever been on a roller coaster? Do you remember that feeling when you climb the first tall hill before reaching the top? Maybe it's fear? Maybe excitement? Or suspense? All three? For Merle and Dave, it felt a lot like being carried up into the air by a harrier, an experience they did not care to repeat.

"I don't like up!" Merle yelled. The guards' log also came to a clanking stop at the base of the hill before starting its ascent.

"Up isn't as bad as down," Pearl noted philosophically.

"What do we do?" Merle fretted, danger ahead and behind.

"We hang on!" Pearl shouted as the log crested the hill.

CHAPTER 20

"Now for a little clean-up work, Dusty." Delilah smirked. "And I have a bone to pick with you, *Ham*."

"Hee-haw—so funny," Ham said.

"Clever," Dusty replied dryly. "I feel like you've rehearsed that."

When all the animals made a run for it, Delilah targeted and pursued the donkeys, knowing that they helped inform the Gomezes right under her nose. She now had Dusty and Ham cornered with a lasso in hand.

"Sneaky beasts!" she snarled. "I've got a donkey-go-round with your names on it." Nothing is more boring and embarrassing for a donkey than to be forced to walk around in circles all day with crying little kids on his back. Dusty had recently experienced that horror before being rescued by Rebecca and brought to Donkey Haven.

"You wouldn't!" Dusty protested.

"I would!" Delilah barked. "And maybe you'll think twice next time about keeping secrets from me."

"Hmm . . ." a voice sounded.

"I'm glad you agree," Delilah gloated.

"We didn't agree with anything," Ham replied.

"Hmm . . ."

the voice sounded again. Delilah whipped around to find Adriana with a snake in her teeth. With a casual flick of the head, the alpaca released Scarlett, who flew directly into Delilah's face.

"AHHHHHH!" Delilah screamed. "I hate snakes!!!" As she struggled to remove the serpent, she dropped her lasso.

"You're not ssso hot yourself," Scarlett coolly said, tangling herself in Delilah's hair and wrapping around Delilah's shoulders as the donkeys and alpaca ran off.

CHAPTER 21

AHHHHH!

Merle, Pearl, and Dave screamed in
unison as they plummeted toward
a wall of water at the bottom of the
flume. With their front paws, they
clung on to the safety bar for dear life
as their back paws trailed in the air
behind.

"We're gonna hit!" Pearl hollered
in horror.

"It's gonna hurt!" Dave yelled.

Have you been wondering why the
ride is named Red Sea Rapids? Remember the story from Exodus in the Bible
when the Israelites were running from

the Egyptian army? Moses stretched out his hand over the Red Sea and God sent a wind to part the waters.

With the Red Sea Rapids, all it took was the press of a button by the ride operator.

"Fear not," Ruben said as he pressed a button marked *PART*. Immediately, the water over the track split in two and opened a dry, clear path for the log to zoom through.

"WOO-HOO!" Merle, Pearl, and Dave shouted as they zipped through the passage—watery walls on either side. "Somebody's watching out for us!" Merle exclaimed.

Do you remember the other part of the Exodus story? When the Egyptian army followed after?

"Haha!" shouted the guards in the pursuing log as it crested the hill and plummeted down toward the divided waters—the squirrels squarely in their sights.

Ruben's finger hovered over a button marked *UN-PART*.

As the squirrels' log followed the track up another hill above water level, the guards' log entered the watery channel.

"We've got you now!" the guard in the front shouted.

"Do you?" Ruben questioned and pressed the button. Immediately, the watery walls collapsed in on the track, completely engulfing the guards' log so it jolted to a halt. *WHOOSH!*

A splash of water rose high into the air. Still seated and locked into their restraints, the guards' four wet heads emerged just above water level. Fortunately for them, unlike the Red Sea, the pool wasn't very deep.

"I think we lost them!" Merle exclaimed as their log rounded the final curve and came to a stop at the ride's end.

"But you didn't lose me!" Dr. Simon proclaimed, standing in wait on the departure platform.

CHAPTER 22

"Where are Merle and Pearl?!" Michael asked as he, Justin, and Sadie met up with his family outside of the park.

"And where are the donkeys, Dave, and Adriana?" Mrs. Gomez wondered as other escaping talking animals flowed out around them and scattered into the surrounding hills.

"Maybe they got lost?" Jane wondered.

"Or worse—" Dr. Gomez fretted.

"—recaptured?" Sadie finished for him.

"We've got to find them!" Justin said.

"Agreed." With Dr. Gomez at the

lead, they all turned and ran back into BabbleLand.

You'll notice on any map of the Holy Land that the Red Sea lies just south of the Dead Sea. BabbleLand was no different. As the squirrels and Dave jumped off the Red Sea Rapids to escape Dr. Simon, they headed through the Withered Wilderness and found themselves entering Dead Sea Shores.

"Oh no! Not the Dead Sea again!" Merle huffed, out of breath. "How is this an attraction?!!!"

"It's not so bad," Dave replied. "It's a dry heat."

"I'm disappointed you don't approve, Merle," Dr. Simon gasped

in chase. "Hurts . . . my feelings, really.
. . . I've worked so hard."

The squirrels stopped short at the
entrance to an artificial cave. A hinged
gate stood open on one side of the
rocky entrance, like a jail cell.

"I'm not going in there!" Merle
cried.

"There's nowhere else to run!" Pearl said. They were, as they say, between a rock and a hard place. Or between a caged cave and a crazed curator.

"Smart squirrel!" Dr. Simon grinned. "Welcome home! It shouldn't take too long to adjust. Sleep in the cave at night, and in the morning be greeted with the petting hands of adoring fans!"

"Stop it!" Merle pleaded. "I'm not the touchy-feely type!"

Dr. Simon crept closer, his long, bony, grabby fingers outstretched. "Now why don't you all get some sleep. . . . It's been a long day," he offered ominously as he bent down toward the frightened critters.

"Why don't you?!" Michael shouted as he emerged behind Dr. Simon along with Justin and Sadie. With a shove, Michael pushed the bent-over baddie forward, past the squirrels and into the cave. As Dr. Simon landed with a thud on the soft sandy soil, Justin and Sadie slammed the gate closed!

"Nice work, kids." Ruben smiled proudly from the control room before pressing the *ALL LOCK* button.

CHAPTER 23

"Father Phillip! What are you doing here?!" Michael exclaimed as the Gomezes and friends exited the park at the maintenance gate.

"I came to get my van back!" the friendly friar replied from the driver's seat of the church van the family had been using to traipse around Israel. "I'll need it for Holy Week at the basilica. A lot going on—and I got a text from Ruben that your mission is complete?"

"That is correct," Ruben announced, emerging from BabbleLand. "However, I suggest the Gomezes and the squirrels

get out of the country before Dr. Simon
gets out of his cave."

The kids all rushed to hug their
former rival. "Thank you, Ruben!"
Michael, Justin, and Sadie said in
unison.

"And before Delilah gets out of her snake," Dusty added.

"What?!" Mrs. Gomez gasped.

"Hmm . . ." Adriana hummed with a smile.

"Don't worry. She'll be fine. She's too big to eat," Dusty reassured them.

"And a little too bitter," Ham added.

"What about you guys?" Merle asked the donkeys, Adriana, and Dave. "How are you going to fit on the plane?"

"You could hide me in a backpack," Dave said. "But I doubt I'd make it past security."

Justin glanced at Michael. "You'd be surprised," he said.

"I could use some help at the basilica!" Father Phillip said. "You could come with me back to Nazareth!"

"Deal!" agreed Dusty. Nazareth was home, after all, to both him and Ham.

"Hmm . . ." agreed Adriana. Anywhere with Dusty was good enough for her.

"Maybe you can drop me off near Jericho later?" asked Dave. "I'm more of a desert lizard."

"You got it!" Father Phillip confirmed.

"We had you all wrong, Ruben. We can't thank you enough," Dr. Gomez said, holding out his hand.

"We couldn't have done this without your help," Mrs. Gomez said.

"Well, *I* was the one who was all wrong, but thank you for your kindness. You are a nice family," Ruben said, shaking Dr. Gomez's hand as

Pearl hugged his ankle. "And squirrels," he added.

"You're not so bad yourself," Merle said, offering Ruben a miniature high five. "As squirrelnappers go, you're one of the good ones."

"And as a tormenting rodent, you are definitely in the top ten," Ruben ribbed.

"If you're done with goodbyes," Debbie announced before landing on Ruben's shoulder, "I suggest we all get out of here while the getting is good!"

"Debbie!" Jane cheered.

"What are you gonna do, Ruben?" Michael wondered.

"Who knows?" Ruben admitted. "But I've got a friend to help me figure it out," he said, patting the cockatoo on the head.

And with that, they all loaded into the van and tow-behind donkey cart. Ruben and Debbie walked off into the night as Father Phillip pulled out of the empty BabbleLand parking lot toward Tel Aviv.

CHAPTER 24

It was an odd sight at Tel Aviv's international airport that evening. As Father Phillip pulled the van into the departures drop-off, the typical flurry of travelers exiting cabs and exchanging hugs with family members was joined by a cacophony of tears, squeaks, hums, and hee-haws. Finally, the Gomezes, Justin,

Sadie, and two emotional-support-vest-wearing squirrels headed into the terminal.

"Don't be strangers!" Dusty called out from the trailer as the van pulled away. "I mean, hee-haw!" he corrected at the looks of astonished bystanders.

"Hope to see you again soon!" Dave shouted from the rolled-down passenger window.

Other than Michael again forgetting he had a full bottle of water in his backpack and making a security agent cranky, getting through security and onto the plane was uneventful.

"Pretzels or nuts?" a familiar flight attendant asked before noticing the squirrels. "You have emotional support squirrels, too?! So adorable! It must be a new thing."

Pearl smiled politely, and Merle whispered something to Sadie.

"He'll have the nuts," Sadie said as Merle held out his paws expectantly.

Shocked, the flight attendant tossed out a bag of nuts before quickly continuing back down the aisle.

"We're going home, guys!" Michael said from his seat next to Justin across the aisle.

"This was quite the adventure!" Pearl proclaimed.

"I've had my fill of adventure," Merle noted. "I'm looking forward to getting back home and relaxing!"

"You do realize there is a cat at home who wants to eat us?" Pearl replied.

"Cats I can handle," Merle said. "Besides, I kind of miss Mr. Nemesis."

"I miss him too!" Jane said through the crack of the seat behind the squirrels.

"I'm glad we finally got the chance to visit Israel as a family!" Mrs. Gomez said.

"Hopefully next time, we won't be in such a rush," Dr. Gomez noted. "Believe me, there is so much more to see!"

"I believe," Merle said, opening up the bag of almonds. "When do they serve dinner?"

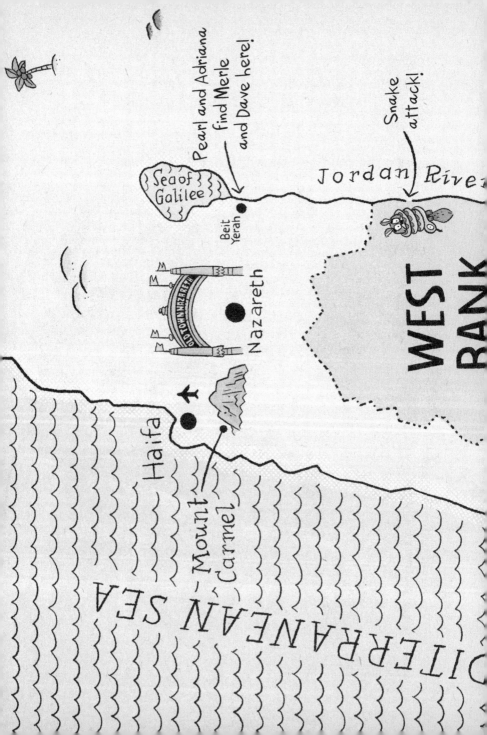

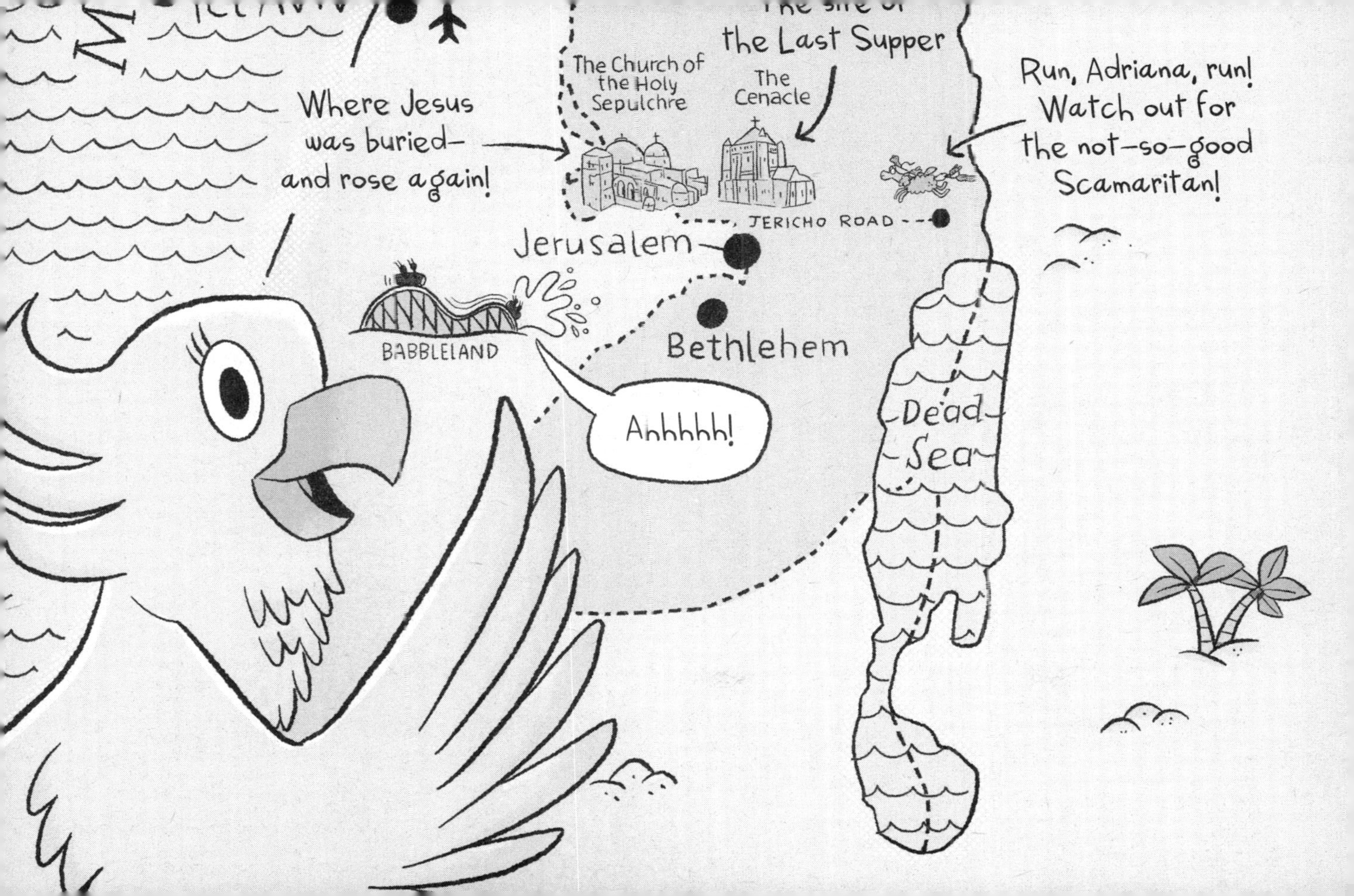
the Last Supper
The Church of the Holy Sepulchre
The Cenacle
Where Jesus was buried—and rose again!
Run, Adriana, run! Watch out for the not-so-good Scamaritan!
JERICHO ROAD
Jerusalem
BABBLELAND
Bethlehem
Ahhhhh!
Dead Sea

MICHAEL GOMEZ is an adventurous and active 10-year-old boy. He is kindhearted but often acts before he thinks. He's friendly and talkative and blissfully unaware that most of his classmates think he's a bit geeky. Michael is super excited to be in fifth grade, which, in his mind, makes him "grade school royalty!"

MERLE SQUIRREL may be thousands of years old, but he never really grew up. He has endless enthusiasm for anything new and interesting—especially this strange modern world he finds himself in. He marvels at the self-refilling bowl of fresh drinking water (otherwise known as a toilet) and supplements his regular diet of tree nuts with what he believes might be the world's most perfect food: chicken nuggets. He's old enough to know better, but he often finds it hard to do better. Good thing he's got his wife, Pearl, to help him make wise choices.

PEARL SQUIRREL is wise beyond her many, many, many years, with enough common sense for both her and Merle. When Michael's in a bind, she loves to share a lesson or bit of wisdom from Bible events she witnessed in her youth. Pearl's biggest quirk is that she is a nut hoarder. Having come from a world where food is scarce, her instinct is to grab whatever she can. The abundance and variety of nuts in present-day Tennessee can lead to distraction and storage issues.

JUSTIN KESSLER is Michael's best friend. Justin is quieter and has better judgment than Michael, and he is super smart. He's a rule follower and is obsessed with being on time. He'll usually give in to what Michael wants to do after warning him of the likely consequences.

SADIE HENDERSON is Michael and Justin's other best friend. She enjoys video games and bowling just as much as cheerleading and pajama parties. She gets mad respect from her classmates as the only kid at Walnut Creek Elementary who's not afraid of school bully Edgar. Though Sadie's in a different homeroom than her two best friends, the three always sit together at lunch and hang out after class.

DR. GOMEZ, a professor of anthropology,
is not thrilled when he finds out that his son,
Michael, smuggled two ancient squirrels home
from their summer trip to the Dead Sea, but
he ends up seeing great value in having them
around as original sources for his research.
Dad loves his son's adventurous spirit but
wishes Michael would look (or at least peek)
before he leaps.

MRS. GOMEZ teaches part-time at her daughter's preschool and is a full-time mom to Michael and Jane. She feels sorry for the fish-out-of-water squirrels and looks for ways to help them feel at home, including constructing and decorating an over-the-top hamster mansion for Merle and Pearl in Michael's room. She also can't help but call Michael by her favorite (and his least favorite) nickname, Cookies.

MR. NEMESIS is the Gomez family cat who becomes Merle and Pearl's true nemesis. Jealous of the time and attention given to the squirrels by his family, Mr. Nemesis is continuously coming up with brilliant and creative ways to get rid of them. He hides his ability to talk from the family, but not the squirrels.

JANE GOMEZ is Michael's little sister. She's super adorable but delights in getting her brother busted so she can be known as the "good child." She thinks Merle and Pearl are the cutest things she has ever seen in her whole life (next to Mr. Nemesis) and is fond of dressing them up in her doll clothes.

RUBEN, previously known only as "the man in the suit and sunglasses," has been on the squirrels' tails ever since Michael discovered them at the Dead Sea. Ruben is determined to capture and deliver the refugee rodents to his boss in Israel. He's clever and inventive, but then again, so are the squirrels! Ruben struggles to stay one step ahead of Merle and Pearl.

DR. SIMON is the director of the Jerusalem Antiquities Museum and Ruben's boss. The mastermind behind the creation of the world's first and largest talking-animal petting zoo, he'll stop at nothing to make sure Merle and Pearl headline the grand opening of his theme park alongside a bevy of other babbling biblical beasts.

FATHER PHILLIP is a kind and helpful friar who first encounters Merle and Pearl at the Basilica of the Annunciation in Nazareth. He becomes a trusted local ally of Dr. Gomez and Michael, keeping an ear to the ground for the whereabouts of the squirrels as they are smuggled about Israel.

ADRIANA hails from South America (like all alpacas), so how did she end up in Israel? No one knows for sure, but what is certain is that Adriana is the best friend a donkey could ask for and president of the Dusty Fan Club. She can't speak, but she can pick locks with her lips and has a knack for being in the right place at the right time.

DUSTY is a retired Holy Land tour donkey, purchased by Ruben for agorot on the shekel (pennies on the dollar) to transport Merle and Pearl from Galilee to Judea. The squirrels soon discover that Dusty can also speak human and is a direct descendant of Balaam's donkey of biblical fame.

DELILAH is the director of Old Town Nazareth, a living history park in Nazareth, Israel. When she's not demonstrating how to use first-century tools or how to weave sheep's wool, she's secretly working with Dr. Simon to capture talking animals for display at BabbleLand in Jerusalem. She also has her eye on Ruben's job as Dr. Simon's right-hand man (er . . . woman) and is every bit as scheming as her biblical namesake.

DAVE is a Lizard of Judah, a talking lizard
native to the Judean Desert (between Jerusalem
and the Dead Sea). Dr. Simon believes Dave's
cheerful bright-blue color and optimistic
demeanor will make him a BabbleLand tourist
magnet—if only Dr. Simon could catch him!
Dave's favorite treat is locusts and honey, and
his keen nose for the sweet treat leads him to
Merle. The two become fast friends and dedicated traveling buddies.

DR. GOMEZ'S
Historical Handbook

So now you've heard of the Dead Sea Squirrels, but what about the
DEAD SEA *SCROLLS*?

Way back in 1946, just after the end of World War II, in a cave along the banks of the Dead Sea, a 15-year-old boy came across some jars containing ancient scrolls while looking after his goats. When scholars and archaeologists found out about his discovery, the hunt for more scrolls was on! Over the next 10 years, many more scrolls and pieces of scrolls were found in 11 different caves.

There are different theories about exactly who wrote on the scrolls and hid them in the caves. One of the most popular ideas is that they belonged to a group of Jewish priests called Essenes, who lived in the desert because they had been thrown out of Jerusalem. One thing is for sure—the scrolls are very, very old! They were placed in the caves between the years 300 BC and AD 100!

Forty percent of the words on the scrolls come from the Bible. Parts of every Old Testament book except for the book of Esther have been discovered.

Of the remaining 60 percent, half are religious texts not found in the Bible, and half are historical records about the way people lived 2,000 years ago.

The discovery of the Dead Sea Scrolls is one of the most important archaeological finds in history!

OLD JERUSALEM

CHURCH OF THE
HOLY SEPULCHRE

MUSLIM
QUARTER

CHRISTIAN
QUARTER

PREVIOUS
SITE OF TEMPLE

DOME OF
THE ROCK

TEMPLE
MOUNT

ARMENIAN
QUARTER

JEWISH
QUARTER

ZION
GATE

CENACLE

Everybody likes a little history lesson, right?!
You might be wondering why the Old City
of Jerusalem is divided into four quarters—
actually four quarters and a mount.

Here's why:

About 3,000 years ago (1,000 years *before* Jesus was born), King David made Jerusalem the capital of Israel. King David's son, the wise King Solomon, built the first Temple—the dwelling place of God on earth and the spot where the Ark of the Covenant rested. A few hundred years later, King Nebuchadnezzar of Babylon destroyed the Temple and scattered many of the Jewish people into other lands. But 50 years after that, the Jewish leader Ezra led the rebuilding of the second Temple, which, once completed, stood for nearly 500 years. It's easy to understand why there's a Jewish Quarter in the Old City.

Jesus visited the second Temple many times to teach and pray. He served his Last Supper, was crucified, buried, and rose from the dead in areas near the Temple. Many of his followers (called Christians) continued to live in Jerusalem. About 40 years after Jesus' life on earth, the Romans, like Nebuchadnezzar before them, destroyed the Temple.

Followers of the religion of Islam, also known as Muslims, believe that their founder

Muhammad ascended into heaven in the year 621 (over 600 years *after* Jesus was born) at the very same location as the first and second Temples. Soon after, Muhammad's followers took control of Jerusalem and built the Dome of the Rock on the site known as the Temple Mount. It was rebuilt in 1023, and that building stands to this day. In 1535 (about 100 years before the first Pilgrims landed at Plymouth Rock), Muslims enclosed the Old City within walls.

Whew! Are you still following? We've got Jews, we've got Christians, we've got Muslims, and we've got the Temple Mount. What about the Armenians? Armenians are originally from a country called—you guessed it—Armenia! Armenia is located between Turkey and Iran (about 800 miles from Israel). Many Armenians became Christians around the year 300 (300 years after Jesus and 300 years before Muhammad) and moved to Jerusalem to become part of the Christian community there. In recent history—the early 1900s—when your great-great-grandparents were around, thousands of Armenians fled to

151

Jerusalem during World War I to escape being killed.

So, there you have it! The Jewish Quarter, the Christian Quarter, the Muslim Quarter, and the Armenian Quarter—all within the tall walls of the Old City and separated into four traditional religious/ethnic neighborhoods. Add to that the Temple Mount with the Dome of the Rock and you've got the Old City of Jerusalem. Aren't you glad you learned so much history?!

About the Author

As co-creator of VeggieTales, co-founder
of Big Idea Entertainment, and the voice
of the beloved Larry the Cucumber,
MIKE NAWROCKI has been dedicated
to helping parents pass on biblical
values to their kids through storytelling
for over two decades. Mike currently
serves as assistant professor of film and
animation at Lipscomb University in
Nashville, Tennessee, and makes his
home in nearby Franklin with his wife,
Lisa, and their two children. The Dead
Sea Squirrels is Mike's first children's
book series.